For Peter
who moved to Maastricht
with much love
Viv

For Tiff
R.C.

Published exclusively for
J Sainsbury plc
Stamford Street, London SE1 9LL
by Walker Books Ltd
87 Vauxhall Walk
London SE11 5HJ

First published 1994

2 4 6 8 10 9 7 5 3

Text © 1994 Vivian French
Illustrations © 1994 Robert Crowther

Printed in Great Britain

ISBN 0-7445-3528-X

Little Red Car to the Rescue

Written by
Vivian French

Illustrated by
Robert Crowther

SAINSBURY'S   WALKER BOOKS

"B'rrrr!" The little red car shivered. It was pouring with rain, and he felt cold and wet and miserable. He was parked outside Gran's flat, and he could just see into the warm, cosy kitchen where Gran and Polly were playing cards.

"It's all right for them," thought the little red car crossly. "They're nice and dry, but I have to stay out here in the rain all night. B'rrrrrrr!"

B'rrrrrr!

"WOORRAWOORRAWOORA!" The little red car heard a strange noise. "WOORA … WOOR … WOR…"

"That's Mrs Lee's blue car," thought the little red car to himself. "At least, I think it is. It sounds very poorly."

Bang! Mrs Lee slammed the door of the blue car, and came hurrying up to Gran's front door. She was carrying something wrapped in a blanket.

RRRRING! "That's Gran's doorbell," thought
the little red car. "I wonder what's going on?"
Gran opened the door, and the little red car
could see Polly peeping out of the kitchen
window.

"Please can you help me?" Mrs Lee sounded very
anxious. "My baby has a very nasty cough and I
have to get some medicine from the chemist –
and my car just won't start."

"Of course we'll help. My car ALWAYS starts,"
said Gran. The little red car gulped. He was
feeling terribly damp – would he really be able
to help?
He wasn't even sure if he liked babies very
much. They left squelchy bits of biscuit all
over his nice clean seats.

GULP!

Gran and Polly hurried out of the flat in scarves and hats. Polly helped Mrs Lee and the baby into the back of the little red car, and Gran jumped into the driving seat.

"Don't cry, baby," said Polly. "We'll soon get your medicine."

The little red car was worried. The baby was
coughing now, and everybody was depending
on him – but could he really start?
Gran turned the key.

"Er … er … er…" said the little red car.
"Oh dearie, dearie me," said Mrs Lee.
"The shops will be shut in a minute…"

"Come on, little red car," said Polly. "You can do it!"
"Yes," thought the little red car, "YES – I CAN!"

"Er … er … B'RRRRRRRM! B'RRRRRRRM!"
His engine roared into life.
"Hurrah!" shouted Polly.

The little red car hurried in and out of the traffic
in the wet streets. He scurried past buses and
lorries, and round the roundabout.

"We're nearly there," said Mrs Lee. "It's just at
the end of this road. I can see the lights – OH!
OH! The lights have gone out!"

Everyone looked at the shop. As they drove
towards it a man came out, carrying a big bunch
of keys.

"Toot toot!" said the little red car. "Toot toot!"
The man didn't look up. He turned round to
shut the door.

"It's no good," said Mrs Lee, "we're too late."

"I'll make him listen this time," thought the little red car. "I really will… TOOT! TOOOOOOOOT!" Even Polly and Gran gasped. The man was so shocked that he dropped his keys on the pavement, just as the little red car screeched to a stop.

Polly scrambled out of the little red car.
"Please don't lock the door," she said.
"We've come to collect some medicine
for a very ill baby."

The man scratched his head.
"My goodness," he said. "You're only just in time.
If you hadn't hooted so loudly you'd have been
too late."

All the way home Mrs Lee kept thanking Gran and Polly.

"The baby'll soon be all right now," she said.

"But I don't know what I'd have done if it hadn't

been for you and your wonderful little red car."
The little red car felt very proud. He drove very
carefully all the way back to the flats, and
stopped just under the kitchen window as usual.

Mrs Lee and the baby got out, and Polly and Gran
locked the little red car up safely for the night.
The baby had stopped crying, and was looking
at the little red car.
"Car," she said. "Nice car."

"That," said the little red car to himself, "is a very SENSIBLE baby." And he settled down happily for the night.